AF295448

Narrated by the French trader Benoist Rousseau

Translated by: Cherry Chapman

https://www.cherrychapman.com

ROBIN HOOD
WAS A TRADER

ROBIN HOOD WAS A TRADER

BENOIST ROUSSEAU

JDH Editions

Publisher: JDH Editions for Edico
77600 Bussy-Saint-Georges.
Printed by BoD – Books on Demand, Norderstedt, Germany

ISBN: 979-10-91879-68-2
Legal Deposit: June 2019

ACKNOWLEDGMENTS

I want to thank the members of the Andlil forum and everybody on the internet that has encouraged and supported me during all these years.

This book is dedicated to them.

Benoist Rousseau

A trader working for his own account

Founder of the website Andlil.com

https://www.andlil.com

It's a blog about the stock market and the economy in which he shares his passion for trading, his economic analysis and his vision on the evolution of society.

https://www.andlil.com/forum/

It's a very active stock market forum where thousands of traders and internet users come to share their knowledge about the stock market, economy, trading…

Published by JDH Editions

In relation with trading…

Devenez Trader Pro!
(Become a Trader Pro!)
By Benoist Rousseau (May 2019)

Réussir en bourse, c'est presque facile !
(Succeeding in the stock market, it's almost easy!)
By Jean-David Haddad, editor in chief of France-bourse.com (January 2017)

Le trading, c'est presque facile !
(Trading, it's almost easy!)
By Stéphane Ceaux-Dutheil (May 2017)

In relation to other subjects…

Money Game
By Sébastien Thiboumery (February 2019)

L'intelligence artificielle va-t-elle nous tuer?
(Will artificial intelligence kill us?)
By Jean-Claude Bourret (November 2017)

La révolution technologique qui va bientôt nous surprendre (The technological revolution that will soon surprise us)
By Fréderic Granotier and Christophe Jurczak (May 2018)

Foreword

The term "trader" comes from the English word "trade" which means "exchange, commerce". A trader is an individual who trades financial products on behalf of a bank or brokerage firm. His job is to buy and resell, buy and resell, to infinity and often in a very short time.

In fact, the author is not a trader working for an institution but rather for his own account. He clearly differentiates between these two major categories of traders.

Through a narrative, a kind of written short-movie recounting of a real scene, Benoist Rousseau explains how, by going to a simple neighbors' party, he could be stigmatized and cause questioning or rejection as soon as he presents himself as a trader. This stigma is often due to people's lack of knowledge regarding the profession of a trader.

It is through crisp dialogues and with a dose of humor that Benoist Rousseau, explaining his daily trader life, his way of life in opposition to the social norm, comes to the simultaneously provocative but unstoppable conclusion that a trader working for his own account is actually a Robin Hood.

Neighbors Day

I had been a tenant in a building of 20 apartments for three months and I had almost never come across my neighbors. A few stealthy encounters at the mailboxes, a quick hello, a gesture of civility to hold the door behind me, a smile, it was about all of the social relations that I could have made. And it was fine by me. I love silence and solitude, eremitism attracts me, I rarely leave my house and I am by no means in search of new friends, I already have too many...

One morning, just like any other, I found an invitation in my mailbox:

"We are organizing a Neighbors Day and your presence is desired. Please indicate if you will be bringing something to eat and/or to drink".

Bla-bla.

I hesitated for a while because this kind of party, where everyone smiles to each other all the while judging them silently to then ramble about them later, was not really my cup of tea. I'm not really curious about the lives of others, but there are some mandatory passages in life, and presenting myself is the least I can do. Being the new tenant in a building of owners, living on the top floor in the largest apartment, I clearly must apologize for this disruption in the hierarchy of norms. An unshaven hermit tenant living above the co-owners, this was enough to create queries or even concerns. I saw some suspicious and questioning looks; my sloppy appearance was not helping me at all. It was final, I was going out of my den. And there I was with my salad bowl filled with assorted salads of varying quality, bread and homemade pesto from basil, that was freshly washed, leveled and cut. I had put on my best jeans (the one with no holes in it) and I was standing at the foot of the building with my housing comrades. I wanted to make a good impression, surely due to my classical education.

The buffet was already set on wooden trestles and cheap garden lounges. The culinary spaces were well defined: large salad bowls of various chips, a mountain of charcuterie, quiches and homemade desserts (note for tonight: think to compliment the pastry chefs without marking any preference).

The next famine seems far away. I will be putting on another 2 kilos after this. Oh, I think there is a famine in Somalia right now? I don't remember, I think I saw it passing on a BFMTV banner between football results and the weather. There must have been enough food for 5 days on the tables and enough drinks for 15.

I spotted a forsaken water bottle from the corner of my eye. I don't drink alcohol. People always ask me about this social anomaly in the country of Rabelais. "You don't drink?" My response varies, according to my mood of the moment, from a guilt response such as "I cannot, I have liver cirrhosis" to a replica that immediately creates social ties such as "I cannot, I had too much to drink yesterday". But generally, I pretend to drink Vodka with a glass of water so as not to disturb my hosts or pass for a miserable teetotaler.

The reception was nice, almost warm. People were somewhat all over me, I was the attraction, the novelty for these co-owners who knew each other for a long time and who have little to say to one another. I'll jump right into the questions. Where did you live before? Are you originally from the region? How did you find this apartment?

I skillfully slipped in that I was delighted with the quality of the building and its environment although, unfortunately, I don't have the chance to be an owner but rather a simple tenant. It delighted them. My integration process seemed to be going on the right track right up to the question that I feared:

And what is it you do in life?

I Am a Trader Working for My Own Account

"I've had a lot of jobs: market salesman, farm worker… I worked for a multinational oil company as a business historian, then for a large international group as a computer trainer and, above all, I taught ten years as a professor of history and geography, but ever since I resigned from my position at the Department of Education, I have been a trader working for my own account".

There it was, I had dropped the bomb. I am a trader. My interest-free professional title was intended to lessen the blast. We'll see what will come of that. At the same time, I'm not looking for an easy way out. Many traders working for their own account elude the question saying they are information technology freelancers and they work at home. This avoids having to explain or justify, but I was in a good mood that night.

An angel passed. The discomfort was palpable. I smiled stupidly, I'm used to it, and I was waiting for the flood.

The first cynical remark was classic, it came from a young neighbor in his thirties, a business owner filing for bankruptcy. He had launched the eighth e-commerce shop in the city believing he would ride the wave. The recall of payroll taxes was fatal, as it often is in the third year of exercise. I would have recommended that he read Schumpeter.

"Well, do you have a Porsche then?" he said ironically with a smile.

"Not at all, I have an old Ford."

And I added, playfully: "Besides I'm a little ashamed, in the residence's garage, there are only BMWs and Porsches; my car is a little out of place."

"Ah, so the rotten car is yours…"

"Yes, the rotten car is mine," I said jokingly, "I'm not very materialistic, I drive it very rarely."

The second remark arrived. It came from a former English teacher who was now retired. She wore little glasses, had a squinchy face, pulled-back blond hair, and she was a rather "literate" person. I saw her face drop when I announced that I was a trader working for my own account. It seemed she had been struck by abomination, though she didn't cross herself despite her golden cross.

"And why did you leave the Department of Education to become a trader?" she asks with a doubtful pout.

I briefly rethought about the "dormitory" of the teachers' room, the breaking of students, the standardization, Françoise telling me about her exciting weekend even though I didn't ask about it, the union delegate furtively stealing reams of paper after we were told about the restrictions on the number of photocopies… But I also remembered the joy of teaching, the kids from very difficult neighborhoods asking me to continue classes on a Saturday noon in the school's parking lot to know the end of the "story", the treasures of imagination that capture their interest. A little nostalgia passed me by, I passionately loved teaching, but by ethics, I had to leave.

"I had promised myself to resign the day I got bored because once I do, I won't have passionate students anymore. That's what I did, in order to live a new life and become a trader working for my own account."

Also, I didn't quite see myself stagnating another 30 years waiting for a pension that I was able to calculate down to the last euro three decades in advance. I was afraid of becoming neurasthenic, I was suffocating in my small professional box where everything was already planned and codified.

I was going to marry a teacher, we were going to have two kids, we would have been 25 to 30 years in debt for a house, we would have gone on weekends to attend a play at the regional drama center where we would have met our colleagues, we would have had a Labrador and, at the cumulative peak of my professional life, I would have probably cheated on my wife with the music teacher to spice up my incomplete life. But the spice would have been the fear of being caught, rather than the carnal pleasure. The death drive at stake, risking one's "perfect life". But I kept that for myself.

"Well, I've actually spent my entire career as a teacher and I never thought of leaving this job," she said, while slightly looking me up and down.

"That's all to your credit, I did not have that courage," I said, shaking my head slightly while concealing as best I could my growing smile.

Fugitive images came to mind. I thought of some jealous colleagues when I left. Many talk of leaving, as the teachers' room is sometimes transformed into a wall of lamentations, but few actually cross the Rubicon. It's difficult to give up on the gilded cage, from the steady paycheck that comes in every 25th of the month with absolute precision, to the remedial vacations, to one's lifetime employment, to tell oneself that one can burn one's diplomas that required so much effort to obtain, in short, to lose one's peaceful flow of life.

My resignation was a total reset; I made a clean sweep of the past, no possibility of going back. I can still see the struggle to leave the Education Nationale, my supervisor opposing the idea for "the good of the service" and trying to hold me back. Until the last second, the Administration made me sign a discharge in which I certified that I had measured the extent of "my choice and its consequences", to try and make me give in at the last second.

I had about more trouble leaving the Department of Education than actually entering it. We do not leave like that, we do not leave the best job in the world without having a problem. I was aware of setting the wrong example, of being a social traitor in the eyes of many of my former colleagues. There is a spirit of wholeness at the Department of Education.

One of the most beautiful days of my life was when I had passed my teacher's examination, it was the end of my troubles, of small jobs. I would have all I needed to eat, stability, I would teach my passion, be useful. I volunteered to teach in the most difficult neighborhoods where I thought I would be most helpful. It gave meaning to my life.

But one of the best days of my life was also ten years later, the departure. When, after having signed the discharge, I slowly descended the steps from the entrance of the educational board. Free, I felt free. The air did not have the same smell as when I arrived, it had a springy scent, something cheerful and fresh. I still see myself stopping at the bottom of this staircase and looking at the sky with a silly smile, taking a deep breath. Despite the fear of the unknown, I felt like Lazarus coming out of his grave.

There Are Two Types of Traders

An abrupt voice shook me from my sweet meditation.

"And for which bank do you work?" asks another neighbor who has just joined the conversation. He seems interested in the discussion. He is a retired director of a local bank branch.

"I don't work for a bank at all. There are two types of traders. The "classic" trader who obeys his superiors, he manages the funds of the bank or those of the customers of the bank. And then there are traders who work for their own account, who trade their own money and try to take away banks' sustenance on the financial markets. They are very different. One is an employee of a bank, the other is an independent who usually works at home, without any hierarchy."

I stopped for a few seconds, took a shot of water Vodka and looked at my neighbors. By a speedy reinforcement, there were more of them listening to me. Well, we'll have to go all the way now. I got back to the subject.

"A trader working for his own account is simply a business leader. He has saved money, spared it or inherited it, for the lucky ones. This personal capital constitutes his working capital. He will trade this capital to try to generate profits."

"To this end, he will buy financial instruments hoping to resell them with a profit like any trader. A merchant buys his apples for € 0.99 to resell them to his customers for € 1.99.

A trader will buy the NASDAQ index at 6,000 from a trader to try to resell it for 6,002 to another trader. If he succeeds, he has gained 2 points. If he fails, he will sell his NASDAQ index at a loss. He is a simple trader who tries to buy a product and resell it for a higher price, like all merchants."

"If he manages to earn money from his buying and selling, he will pay taxes on his profits, just like the grocer or the tobacconist around the corner. And if he ever loses his working capital, he would have nothing left, he would be ruined. A trader working for his own account is a business leader. He has no right to unemployment if he fails he goes directly to the bottom of the scale. I will not go out in front of a town hall to protest and ask for subsidies or help. Like any business owner, I will take the risk that I took and I will start from scratch trying to bounce back."

"So it's a risky choice; I left a job guaranteed for life for this adventure. I do not have a Porsche or an expensive suit, I ride in an old car and I try every month to earn my old salary without any guarantee. I can work all month and still be in the red. And my paid holidays, of course, I don't have them anymore. But it's worth it, I gave up my gilded cage to become free." I concluded.

Wage-Earning is a Modern Serfdom

"Are you freer? Without holidays?" my old colleague asks.

I was sure she was going to reply. I confess, I taunt her a little but I like her, she is a pleasant stinging reminder of my old life. The only thing that bothers me is her gold cross that is too conspicuous. After all, she probably taught in the private sector or hid it in class? This was a pure reflex from a teacher of the public sector, it made me smile.

"Yes, I always considered that working for others is an alienation of one's freedom. The employment contract is nothing less than a temporary serfdom contract. In return for a salary, you partially give up your freedom. One leases one's physical and/or intellectual workforce to a boss, an institution or a government for a precise duration. During this period of time, one is no longer free of one's movements, choices, and decisions."

"When I was a teacher, my schedule, the educational curricula and the date of my vacations were imposed on me. I had no real freedom of action. Of course, we had work meetings where everyone pretended to believe that our remarks would be heard in the development of school programs, for example. It was the illusion of direct democracy. We filled our registers of grievances, then distant authorities set the program, and, in theory, I had to apply it submissively and uniformly to my students."

"When I worked in the private sector, I had to hand in my vacation request and wait for the company's validation. Flexibility helped though, considering my schedule could change from one week to the next. I was selling my free time for pay. I did not belong to myself during those hours. I preferred being an employee because the time was clearly set."

"But when I was an executive, my serfdom contract was amenable to my boss's every whim. I was no longer protected by time limits because I had missions, objectives. And so I brought work home because they managed to make me feel guilty, my space of personal freedom was reduced little by little in favor of my serfdom. The only boundary I had was my own resistance to the company's pressure. There is a kind of perverse game between the company and its executives."

I stopped to catch my breath. I may have gone too far? I looked at my neighbors while taking a virtual Vodka shot. I had trouble deciphering their facial expressions. A neighbor smiled, either he liked me or he saw me as a comic or a jerk. Some faces were sullen, I probably hit too hard with serfdom. It wasn't very clever at all. I could have avoided that part, especially with neighbors who must mostly be executives. I should have made the link with BMWs and other luxury cars surely paid in overtime. I let myself get carried away again. Congratulations on the integration process, I got off to a bad start…

It could have been much worse, it's a good thing I didn't talk about slavery and make the comparison with a cashier working half-time in a shopping center or a pressured executive. Sometimes I wonder, a slave had to work several years, sometimes a decade in order for the master to recover his "initial investment". To this end, he had to keep his slave's workforce intact and therefore not abuse him badly, he had to feed him, house him, take care of him. But what is the company's value in a cashier paid half-time or an executive in a massive unemployment situation? It didn't cost them a cent, it's an interchangeable workforce. A part-time cashier's salary does not allow for food and lodging. This is not the company's problem whilst it sure was the master's. I did well to not to say that, for with alcohol going around, some might have thought I stood for the restoration of slavery. At the same time, what an idiot I was! I was at the neighbors' party, this was not the place to discuss these matters, we are here to relax and drink, not to talk about serfdom. I have again spoiled the mood. And to add: "Now I am completely free. I get up when I want, I work when I want, I have no more authority over me. I no longer suffer the moods of bosses on Monday morning when they had a bad weekend. The only person I have to answer to is myself. And above all, I have a supreme level of freedom, I am fully responsible for my actions. I am no longer disempowered as it was too often the case in my old jobs."

After all, it was the truth! I was the one and only person responsible for my decisions. Nobody imposed choices or decisions on me; if I made money, I owed it only to myself; if

I lost money, I was the only one at fault. That's why it's a difficult job. There are no false pretenses, we cannot lie to ourselves, dilute our responsibility or accuse Pierre, Paul or Jacques of having killed the contract. It is neither the fault of colleagues, nor of the company, nor of superiors, and not the weather outside. We're in it by ourselves. And it's the most beautiful thing in this business and the most difficult because we tend to live in a society of disempowerment. We end up being infantilized in our professional life. Here, we are faced with the raw truth, no excuse possible. I feel like I have become an adult with this job. I don't look for excuses like a teenager, I am master of my success or my failure.

And what a pleasure to no longer wear penguin costumes! It's amazing the sense of freedom that it brings to be liberated from the dress conventions imposed by the world of work," I concluded.

You Speculate on the Lives of Others

"Do you realize that what you do is immoral? You speculate on people's lives with trading! You live off the work of others!" my retired neighbor acclaimed while raising her voice. What about socialists and conservatives? There must be some at this party.

That was the wave I was waiting for, the immoral side of trading, the attack on speculation, the old classic songs. Normally it happens faster, it's not too bad, I could explain in part what I do. Come on, let's attack the tough part, the difficulty of questioning some well-established certainties.

"Yes, that's what we often read or what we're told by many politicians. It's an absolute joke for me because I have absolutely no impact on the lives of businesses and people. I made the choice of having a trade that I would describe as ethical."

"Ethical?..."

"Yes... I trade only indices. Whether buying or selling indices, speculating on inflation or the fall of these indices, this has absolutely no impact on stock prices and therefore on the companies and employees who work there. I do not receive dividends either. I buy and sell an index that is but a weighted average of shares. I have no impact on the real economy, I'm totally "neutral", my carbon footprint is rather excellent seeing that I work at home," I said ironically.

One of the neighbors laughed. I turned to him smiling. He was in his late forties, dressed with care in pants and a linen shirt. I had spotted that he had arrived alone with his little girl of about 8 years old. She just doesn't let go of him, she was stuck to his leg, sometimes hugging him as children would embrace their stuffed animal. What would Dolto have seen in this? He may be divorced and in shared custody, it's the weekend, the story holds up. The trauma seems recent for both of them, the little girl fears further separation by the way she merges with her father's leg. "You won't leave me anymore Dad." He is bored to be there but he seems as polite as I am, he has little choice. In his eyes, there is immense fatigue and sadness. He seems to be a tortured man who is probably a light sleeper. A nice guy. There is still some life in him, his eyes sparkled a few seconds before going out. He smiled at me weakly. End of the complicity. I resumed what I was saying.

"My only real economic impact is to have created my own job with my personal money. I am not waiting for a business owner to start his business or develop in order to hire me or for the state to recruit new staff. It is rather positive in my opinion, I took it in hand, I didn't wait until someone created my employment." I stopped, I found myself to be liberal in my remarks, too liberal. I don't mean that the person who does not create his job is passive; a society of generalized auto-entrepreneurs is not really desirable. I was going to add a little more nuance when I was interrupted.

"But traders speculate on raw materials, they drive up prices!" the retired professor said, more and more annoyed. She started getting pretty upset. Her tone went up, she squeezed her glass of wine a little harder, and her knuckles were slightly white. I doubt she will be inviting me to her house for tea in the next few days. I will try to bring it down a notch by going in her direction. I'll hate myself if I spoiled Neighbors Day.

"Absolutely! But it is impossible to say whether it is negative or positive. For example, let's take a barrel of oil. Speculation drives it up. The Western middle class isn't happy that the price at the gas station rises. But for the producing countries it is a boon, they can develop their country, feed their population, build infrastructure… and they can even absorb the debt issued by the Western countries so that they maintain their standard of living. This is the ultimate paradox!"

"Conversely, when the price of cocoa and coffee falls due to speculation, the Western consumer rejoices while it is a tragedy for producers in Africa. So, is there good or bad speculation? We cannot protest about the rising prices of raw materials that we do not produce and at the same time want the development of poor producing countries. "Some consistency is called for," I said, thinking of a close friend.

This friend has been fighting for the development of poor countries for decades. A committed activist, if not fierce, she is an example of humanism for me. But she is the first to be upset when her coffee acquires 1 € per kilo. Certainly, for her defense, she drinks more than 10 per day, but still.

"In the 1950s and 1960s, we experienced a very strong growth called The Glorious Thirties. You cannot ignore the facts, it was partly due to the fact that we had colonies and therefore raw materials at almost cost price. The pinnacle of our Western growth was made on resources paid very much lower than their real value. Fortunately, globalization has helped rebalance forces (OPEC is a good example) and get 1 billion people out of extreme poverty in recent decades by paying them a fairer price for their natural resources. We live in a much fairer world than in the 1950s and 1960s, when France and the United Kingdom had half of humanity under their colonial control. It is totally illusory to want to return to the golden age of the sixties, of growth fueled by cheap raw materials and full employment. We should resubmit a part of Humanity to under our domination and I have the impression that they won't give up without a fight." I said, thinking of the League of Delos.

The golden age of Athens and the invention of democracy correspond to the league of Delos. Initially, this alliance protected the Greek cities who wished to be protected against the Persian danger. In exchange for tributes or contributions to maintain the Athenian military fleet and pay the balance of payments of citizens, Athens commits to defending the Greek member cities of the league against the next Persian invasion. But the Persians didn't come back and, over time, the danger seemed to be getting further and further away. So why pay?

Some Greek cities wanted to come out of this alliance that has become visibly useless, but Athens couldn't afford to lose the treasure of the league of Delos. It financed its military power and the costs of its democracy. Tributes paid an indemnity to Athenian citizens so that they may attend assemblies or perform their annual jury charge if they have been drawn. The very functioning of Athenian democracy was at stake.

The cities that "forgot" to pay the tribute had the Athenian triremes escort the money-gatherers in order to put some pressure. Athens forbade the minting of money to other cities and imposed the use of the Athenian currency. Athens became a more oppressive force rather than a protective one. The members of the League of Delos had lost their independence.

Do democracies, in order to be full-blown, need to subjugate other countries? Like Athens with the League of Delos, or France and the United Kingdom in the middle of the twentieth century with their colonies?

I had a little chagrin as I look at the bottom of my glass. Too bad it's still fake Vodka.

"But to reject speculation seems to me an incredible hypocrisy, everyone speculates, all the time!" I ended up saying in an act of provocation to clear my mind.

We Are All Speculators

"I have never speculated and I will never do so!" said my straight-laced new friend in her pair of white sandals.

"You speculate without being aware of it. All people are speculators."

"I will not dwell on the fact that if there is a place where we speculate on the lives of people, it is at the Department of Education. After all, what is a class and orientation council? It's a collegial decision of a group of teachers who decide, for example, whether or not their students can be oriented to general high school or better suited for technical high school. Speculation with far-reaching consequences on their future lives. That's what I always hated in this business, how could we assume this right to a person's future? I have never known an omniscient teacher. We speculate on students' lives… it's a power that has always scared me," I said, looking at her with a smile.

She looked me straight in the eyes, it seemed like she was holding her breath, and her pupils were dilated. I doubt she was enjoying herself. I gazed upon her for a few seconds. She was getting fired up but she contained herself, quite the character! I nodded my head as a greeting to my opponent and I launched my retort. Thus far, I stayed on the defensive but it was now time to rock the boat a little.

"But more prosaically, you are all owners of your homes here. To my knowledge, I am the only tenant. So you have thus speculated when buying your property. You have estimated that the building was of quality, that its location was good, and that the neighborhood was proactive. You have made the most rational purchase feasible, especially since it is often the purchase of a lifetime, it's better not to get it wrong. But by investing in the neighborhood, you have mathematically raised real estate prices. I have not yet met a landlord who was hoping to sell his apartment or house with a loss in the next few years. We are in pure speculation with real estate. And the owners who are keen on a positive valuation of their property and a steady increase in rents, they are real speculators. That's why a poor tenant like me has to pay more rent to his landlord from year to year," I said with a laugh.

"Come on, buying a house or a share is not the same thing," said a resident who had just arrived. She was in her early thirties, or at the end of her twenties. She wore a black suit, she must have gotten out of work because the makeup on her eyes was a little smudged, a sign that the day was long. She may be an executive who just finished her week. It was past 9pm, she was able to do free overtime on a Friday evening to close the W file. The subject of real estate seemed to interest her.

She may have a credit of 20 to 25 years given her age if she has borrowed money. In the end, I am probably not the only tenant, some are bank tenants for most of their life.

It's a hell of a drag in a society that will require more and more professional mobility. But it's difficult to break such traditional representations. They were valid when people had a career in the same place for all their life, when there was inflation and you could repay your mortgage in 12 to 15 years. The 1970s and 1980s are now far away, but mentalities have not changed. Now, it takes 25 to 30 years to repay a mortgage and you will have to change jobs from 3 to 8 times in your life and thus be required to have significant geographic mobility in order to find a job. Perhaps this is the price to pay to stay within the "norm"?

When you plan to buy a home, you evaluate a property, a neighborhood, a population dynamics on the sector, employment opportunities etc. You will inquire to find out if there are no public works planned in the coming years such as the construction of a highway for example. You estimate if your property can be easily sold in case you might need to move.

This is what I do with indices all the time, I evaluate them to try to determine if they will go up or down in the next days or weeks.

"We are all speculators," I said.

"Your time horizon is long for real estate, my time horizon is shorter because I have to generate a salary every month, but the intellectual approach, the way of proceeding and the goal are the same."

"To avoid being ripped off," I concluded to my fellow real estate speculators.

People and Financial Morality

"No, I was talking about financial speculation! That of the stock market!" my liberal friend reminded me.

It's always difficult to talk about the stock market to people who have little to no practice in the matter. There have been so many images of Epinal circulated and dwelled upon so many times that they have become truths for the general public. I tried to go easy.

"The vast majority of people who are against stock market speculation have life insurance. There is nothing more speculative than these products. When we study their composition, we see that there is, for instance, Greek debt in these products.

Personally, as a trader working for my own account, I have always refused to speculate on the debt of a country for ethical reasons. That's why I never had life insurance or SICAV. These seemingly simple products are actually complex. They are envelopes of financial assets made up of bonds issued by companies and States of the Eurozone, for example. Very few people are interested in their composition. To which countries or companies do they lend money? People don't know anything about it. As long as it pays more than the classic savings, they lose interest in these questions."

I gave my neighbors a minute to figure this out and then I continued.

"The money left on our current accounts is used by banks to make consumer loans. Sometimes, the people who benefit are at the brink of over-indebtedness and they will pay very high-interest rates."

"So if we study the matter a bit, we realize that we have a real moral question to ask ourselves. The money left in banks or invested in the preferred investments of the French is far from trivial. We all have a moral responsibility by entrusting banks to manage our deposits or the contents of our life insurance. Life insurance assets exceed 1,600 billion euros in France, for example. These are huge sums. And we leave this manna, this power, in the hands of banks without even trying to manage it ourselves. We are like children, we do not even control the fruit of our work, our savings, our efforts. It's almost like we're under guardianship."

"That's why I take great care to leave the absolute minimum on my current accounts so as not to fatten up banks. I don't want my money to be used as consumer loans to people in difficulty. 95% of my assets are with brokers. I have total control of my investments. I cannot bear to be infantilized to such an extent."

I saw perplexity on their faces. They must be like everyone else and have life insurance. The name is reassuring and tranquilizing, almost like a medical prescription. Yes, a medical prescription!

I decided not to ruin the evening and not to go any further in this matter. I will not explain to them that their money does not really belong to them. That's right; in case their bank goes bankrupt, their deposits will be used to repay the creditors. They are in solidarity, with most of them not even knowing it, with the financial health of their bank.

The state can do it too with their life insurance. A small decree signed on a Sunday evening and all their assets above a certain sum will be confiscated to prevent the bankruptcy of the state. They will not even have the time to react. Cyprus has done it recently, but everyone has already forgotten that. I hope that we won't be reminded of it one day… French creditors know about this, and so do our leaders. That's why they continue to lend money to a state on the brink of bankruptcy. Our 2,230 billion of debt is guaranteed by the 1,600 billion deposited by the French in life insurance. This may also be the reason why the state continues to take on debt. So far, so good…

The subject is a little taboo, and it was useless to have them worry because it won't change much anyway. For morale, it's not very good to say that we are forced creditors, the last resort in case of problems.

A Trader Working for His Own Account is a Socialist

"So you don't have any money in the bank?" the former banker asked me, quite taken aback.

I smiled.

"I have the bare minimum, enough for day-to-day operations. But there's worse, I have always lived below my means so I have never been overdrawn. I know, I would not have been a good customer for you, I believe banks are making their profitability on over-drawn customers. I'm a socialist so I don't like banks and I don't want to strengthen major capital by leaving my savings there," I said, laughing.

"You're a socialist?" asked my favorite socialist, aghast.

"A little, of heart. I come from a very modest background. At the age of 15, I was able to go abroad for the first time, thanks to my so-cialist municipality which organized very heavily subsidized trips. I was able to go to Poland for a month in 1989. It was the good days, the Berlin Wall had not fallen yet, and we were going to visit a brotherly country. For the child that I was, it was an amazing gift. And just for that, I'm always grateful to the Socialist government for allowing an ordinary lad to travel east," I said with a smile.

A wave of nostalgia came over me. I could see the initiatory journey beyond the Rhine speeding past, the passage to the GDR with the control of the police arming their Kalashnikovs at us in the bus, which instantly calms a bunch of turbulent teenagers, my first Polish cigarette that had saved me from smoking, our stupidity when we were picky at the face of stone-hard meat while our guests were sacrificing so much for us, bartering with Russian soldiers, swapping Bic razors against military medals and my first loving emotions with my Lorelei, a Hungarian communist living in Krakow.

I came back to reality.

"More seriously, by their very nature, socialists are opposed to the capitalist world. They fight against the excesses of finance, the exorbitant power of banks etc. They think society could work better without banks, without financial institutions… The only problem is that there are only a few Socialists who really fight against banks, others collaborate with capitalist banks by leaving their money there, speculating on the debt of the European countries in difficulty with their life insurance… without even knowing it."

"A trader working for his own account is ultimately a true socialist. He is the only one to fight, step by step, day after day, against "major capital". With technical resources derisory to high-frequency trading, with his microscopic capital, he is the only one to face banks that spew hundreds of billions of euros every day on the financial markets."

"Every euro that I earn on the stock exchange to put gas in my Clio, I mainly yank it from City Group, Goldman Sachs, Hedges Funds etc. Of course, I am well aware that I am, along with other traders working for their own account, zooplankton. The sharks of finance are not even aware of our existence because of how tiny we are. But we try to earn our daily bread day after day at the expense of banks, using our assets: our gray matter and our decision-making speed because we have no hierarchy. I think there is a certain nobility and madness in the activity of trading for your own account. We are the only ones to face the banks face-to-face on their own playing field," I concluded.

I looked at my comrades. No reaction. I probably seemed crazy. My talk must really break the framework of classical representations, these easily identifiable little boxes where everyone must stand with a label and play a role. A well-ordered society, everyone has their place, clearly identifiable. A masked society, Molière would have surely said. It's relaxing and reassuring. According to other people's little boxes, we know if we like them or if we hate them.

But here, explaining that I am a trader fighting against banks, it rendered the choice of the box a little complicated. I became abnormal, literally. First off, a trader does not have a good reputation, and I did nothing to improve this image. It may be time to move on, plus I'm starting to get hungry.

"What if we went to have a little something to eat and drink? I talk a lot, but you can stop me, it's my Latin side, plus the others will end up eating everything."

The anxiety of missing out was still working, we reunited at the buffet. There, a jovial neighbor, in his fifties and slightly balding, cuts into a sausage by explaining that it came from a renowned charcuterie of the city. Besides, he had skimmed all the charcuteries of the sector and it was the best sausage that could be found in the region.

Jérôme Kerviel and the Hatred of Traders

"I heard you're a trader. Do you know Jérôme Kerviel? What do you think of him?" he asked, holding out a slice of sausage with his knife. Facing so much passion, I had to taste it. It was actually good; the ratio of pork and added fat was above average.

"No, I don't know Jérôme Kerviel any more than you do. He was a trader at Société Générale who traded the Dax 30 index like me. This is our only point in common. At best he was my "enemy" on the financial markets since he was an employee for Société Générale whilst I try to take away money from these Goliaths. He spewed billions belonging to the bank whilst I manage my savings."

He stared at me.

"But what I remember from the Kerviel affair is that the policies relayed by the media have stigmatized an entire profession. Traders have become the enemy, they are responsible for all that goes wrong, of the crisis, of unemployment, of inequality, of hunger in the world… It's becoming so cartoonish that we can even suspect traders of being responsible for the increase in obesity in the West, of which I am a proud example," I laughed and thought about my diet the following Monday, like every other Monday.

Meanwhile, I felt a great discomfort, my stomach started to hurt. It wasn't the sausage that didn't set well, but memories of this Kerviel period started coming back. There was a popular hatred against all traders, whoever they are, brutally and uniformly. Hatred is always blind, it seems, but whatever it is, it sure packs a mean punch.

I have been threatened with my life multiple times just because I'm a trader working for my own account. The website Libération.fr had written an article about me at the time of the 2011 crisis, which had generated hateful and insulting comments, to the point of wanting to hang myself. Just because I bought the Dax 30 and sold it, it made me the enemy of the people.

It's true that the speeches of politicians are simplistic and they do not define the situation. Who is responsible for the crisis? Traders. Who is the enemy? Finance. And the crowd cheers. Where should the bonfires be set up for burning witches? I know that the designation of a leader can channel the anxiety of the population. If there is a person responsible, then there is a solution. If there is a solution, then the glory days will return. That's the promise. But there is a danger in playing with people's emotions rather than with their reason.

A Crisis? What Crisis?

"So who is responsible for the crisis if it's not the traders?" he asked, handing me a new slice of sausage.

"I'm interested in your answer," added the retiree from the Department of Education.

Ouch. This was a delicate subject. People preferred to be told what they wanted to hear about this anxiety-provoking theme. Well, I could afford the luxury of saying what I thought seeing that I didn't intend to run for office. I didn't need to give false hope in order to collect votes.

"I will surely shock you but there is no crisis. The crisis does not exist, it is an invention to give hope to the Western middle class that has been experiencing an inexorable decline!"

"An economic crisis is a short moment in history, by definition. But it has been four decades, almost five, in which we have been in crisis. For two generations we have been promised that soon the golden age will return. The growth of the 50s and 60s was absolutely exceptional and unique in the history of humanity. In fact, what we call crisis is simply a normal period of the economy. One of the mistakes we make is having as a comparison the case of Les Trente Glorieuses, which occurred only once throughout 5,000 years of human history."

"We are still living on representation models from the 1960s: full employment, wage increases, the dogma of perpetual growth based on inexhaustible and inexpensive raw materials, on the domination of the world by the West…"

"All of that's over, its time has passed. This period existed in the past, how nice for those who lived it, too bad for those who suffered it. We must open our eyes and stop letting ourselves take comfort in empty promises. We must adapt to the world that is right there in front of us because it's our world and it's a normal world. It's The Glorious Thirties that is abnormal from an economic point of view."

"I was born in 1974, I am a child of "the crisis", and full employment is a utopia for me. My generation no longer believes in infinite growth, we live in a world limited in resources, the population is growing steadily, and we will have to share the pie. We cannot keep everything for ourselves as in the mid-20th century."

"When you divide the wealth, those who have more should yield a little to those who have less. The Western middle class is the richest in the world and it is gradually giving up some of its purchasing power, like my friend who pays more for her coffee even though she rants about it, it's an inexorable process."

"Slowly but surely, people's life expectancy and the overall standard of living are improving. A middle class throughout the world starts appearing little by little which will eventually become standardized. Chinese, Bolivians, French… human beings of equal value will have an equivalent standard of living."

"We cannot behave like in the days of the colonies anymore, and consequently globalization is slowly reducing the gap between countries and people. In 20 years, 1 billion people have come out of extreme poverty, famines are shrinking thanks to global solidarity, and infant mortality has collapsed."

"And although we are officially in crisis, we are generally better off now than in the 60s. Our material comfort is much greater, we work less than before and the time available allows us to watch TV reality shows for entertainment, our life expectancy has increased dramatically, which allows us to assume that we will have time for our Alzheimer's to develop," I said ironically.

"I do not deny that there is poverty and suffering… It's real, tangible and it is a horror for those who live it. But we are progressing, it's better to live at the beginning of the 21st century than at the end of the 20th century for the overwhelming majority of the world population, even the West."

"But what seems dangerous to me is to make the Western middle class believe that the glorious days can come back. It's an absolute lie. This will create a game of extremes and populism. Instead of preparing them for a transition, a change in consumer behavior, we continue to lie to them and to infantilize them."

"What will happen when we are going to announce the end of the crisis, when the economy will softly restart and job creation will take off? Many people will expect to see their lives change. And that's normal, it's been 50 years since they've been told: "Hold on, this is the crisis, but things will be better afterwards." The Western middle class thinks that in case of economic recovery; the golden age of the 60s will return. But there will be almost no difference for them. There will be a few more jobs, but mostly precarious jobs."

"Therefore, in real terms, people will see little improvement in their purchasing power, their standard of living, their lifestyle, but absolutely not what they had been hoping for. This will create big frustrations and disappointed hopes. And since the media will be saying that the situation is better, that we will be seeing positive coverage in this sense, the middle class will feel ripped off and may reach out to the populists who will promise them a minimum wage of € 2,000." I concluded.

Minimalization, a Way Out of the Crisis?

"So what is the way out of the crisis then?" my sausage aficionado asked me, offering me a third piece. I refused with a wave of the hand.

"What is the way out? It's to try to evolve. We live in a world where we feel we are in constant shortage, we always want more, we want to consume more. We feel that in order to be happy we need to buy. Our whole society and advertising push us towards more. This is the foundation of our current economic system, it takes perpetual growth for the system to hold up. For example, Okun's law shows that we need 3% growth to start reducing unemployment. So, we have to create new needs all the time to stimulate growth. We thereby get to be continuously dissatisfied, we buy the iPhone 10 and we are already thinking of the iPhone 11 that will be released in 9 months."

"It's a sort of endless rat race that exhausts us and frustrates us. I am a fan of minimalization," I finally admitted.

"A trader who is a minimalist! That's new," said my friend in amazement.

I smiled and answered "I know… it may seem incongruous, but it's the case. I don't trade to enrich myself but rather to pay for my vital needs. I don't dream of a Rolex 50, a big car, or expensive clothes. I don't live for how people perceive me or for trying to impress my neighbor," I said, thinking of a former neighbor.

In the popular district where I lived, he drove around every Saturday with his BMW in slow motion so that we could admire him. It was his pride, his success, and he eagerly wanted us to see him. That was his happiness. The price he paid though was rather high, he was never able to go on vacation and his apartment ended up being seized. But for a few years, he had the most beautiful car in the neighborhood.

"My way of life is difficult to understand for many people. I don't need to own things to be happy. I am a tenant and I will remain so all my life. I admit that I love a little comfort, so I rent a nice apartment because, as a lay hermit, I spend most of my time there. I'm also an epicurean, if I can afford a gourmet restaurant then it's even better, if it's not possible, then it doesn't matter, a pasta dish with butter is always welcome."

"I think that what creates a lot of anguish and violence in our society is this greed and fear of missing out. Besides if we don't hurry, they will eat all the desserts without us!"

And we went to eat our share…

Epilogue

A couple of days later, I had the pleasure of meeting my socialist neighbor in the street. After some small-talk on the state of our health and the weather over the next few days, she asked me an unexpected question: "But by the way, why don't you have children?"

This was a question that I got asked quite often. I'm in my forties, not too ugly, not too stupid, I have some money, a genetic profile that is quite proper, but, according to social norms, I lacked a couple's life with children in order to be fulfilled and, ideally, a dog. The dog with a beautiful car and the house are very important too. Then my life would be accomplished. The French Dream.

"I made the choice of not having any children for moral and ecological reasons," I replied. She then looked at me as Donald Trump would look at a veggie burger, with amazement. An angel passed. Even two.

"But why?" she stammered.

"I think it would be reasonable to control and limit births to give future generations a future that isn't hell. We reproduce like rabbits in a world with limited resources. So, I made the choice, despite many proposals, not to contribute to overcrowding." I answered ironically.

I paused.

"Without being a fortune-teller, we can "predict" the fall in the purchasing power of the Western middle class. More and more of us are sharing a cake whose size is no longer increasing because resources are running out. The Earth is fed up with us and our irresponsibility." I concluded.

"You are mainly selfish for not wanting children, if there are no more children, then there would be no future!" replied my neighbor, angrily.

I smiled, I knew this speech very well. For me, selfishness is to give in to one's instincts of wanting children without asking ourselves how the child will live the next 90 years? But I never say this. What's the point in saying it?

"Because of my "sacrifice", your grandchildren will live better. I think we are actually witnessing the emergence of a global middle class. The globalization we are experiencing is only the establishment of a socialist utopia by liberalism: everyone on the same level.”

“We must make the giants smaller and make the smaller ones bigger, everyone at the same height, that's true happiness.” the French revolutionaries sang in 1789. The problem is that the giants rarely agree. And the giants now, they're us, the western middle class. And I'm rather afraid, for the children that I won't have, that out of selfishness, even the Socialists of the French middle class will fight to not lower and share the cake. We are moving towards an increasingly violent society if even the socialists don't want to share anymore." I said, slightly smiling.

This was my last discussion with my socialist neighbor. She never spoke to me again and when we came across one another, she totally ignored my greetings. Just like the other neighbors from the party, for whom I had become an outcast.

Table of Contents